Yummy Rhymes

Cover illustration by JON GOODELL

Illustrations by
KRISTA BRAUCKMANN-TOWNS
JANE CHAMBLESS WRIGHT
DREW-BROOK-CORMACK ASSOCIATES
KATE STURMAN GORMAN
JUDITH DUFOUR LOVE
BEN MAHAN
ANASTASIA MITCHELL
ANITA NELSON
ROSARIO VALDERRAMA

Louis Weber, C.E.O.
Publications International, Ltd.
7373 North Cicero Avenue
Lincolnwood, Illinois 60646

Manufactured in U.S.A.

8 7 6 5 4 3 2 1

ISBN: 0-7853-1653-1

PUBLICATIONS INTERNATIONAL, LTD.

Pease Porridge Hot

Pease porridge hot,
Pease porridge cold,
Pease porridge in the pot,
Nine days old.
Some like it hot,
Some like it cold,
Some like it in the pot,
Nine days old.

Polly, Put the Kettle On

Polly, put the kettle on,
Polly, put the kettle on,
Polly, put the kettle on,
We'll all have tea.

Sukey, take it off again,
Sukey, take it off again,
Sukey, take it off again,
They've all gone away.

Start the fire and make the toast,
Put the muffins down to roast,
Start the fire and make the toast,
We'll all have tea.

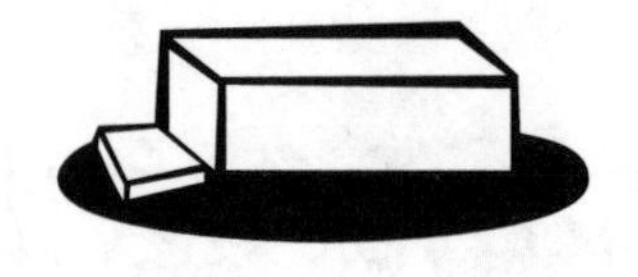

Betty Botter

Betty Botter bought some butter,
But, she said, the butter's bitter;
If I put it in my batter,
It will make my batter bitter,
But a bit of better butter
Will make my batter better.
So she bought a bit of butter,
Better than her bitter butter,
And she put it in her batter
And the batter was not bitter.
So it was better Betty Botter bought
A bit of better butter.

Up in the Green Orchard

Up in the green orchard
   There is a green tree,
The finest of apples
   That you ever did see.
The apples are ripe,
   And ready to fall,
And Reuben and Robin
   Shall gather them all.

Goober and I

Goober and I were baked in a pie,
And it was wonderful hot.
We had nothing to pay
The baker that day
So we crept out and ran away.

Two Make It

Two make it,
Two bake it,
Two break it.

Little Miss Tucket

Little Miss Tucket
  Sat on a bucket,
Eating some peaches and cream.
  There came a grasshopper
Who tried hard to stop her,
  But she said, "Go away, or I'll scream."

An Apple a Day

An apple a day
Sends the doctor away.

Apple in the morning,
Doctor's warning.

Roast apple at night,
Starves the doctor outright.

Eat an apple going to bed,
Knock the doctor on the head.

Three each day, seven days a week,
Rosy apple, rosy cheek.

When Jack's a Very Good Boy

When Jack's a very good boy,
He shall have cakes and custard;
But when he does nothing but cry,
He shall have nothing but mustard.

Green Cheese

Green cheese, yellow laces,
Up and down the marketplaces;
Turn, cheeses, turn.

On Christmas Eve

On Christmas Eve I turned the spit;
I burnt my fingers, I feel it yet;
The sparrow it flew right over the table,
The pot began to play with the ladle;
The ladle stood up like an angry man,
And vowed he'd fight the frying pan;
The frying pan hid behind the door
Said he never saw the like before;
And the kitchen clock I was going to wind,
Said he never saw the like behind.

A Big Fat Bowl of Dumplings

A big fat bowl of dumplings,
Boiling in the pot;
Sugar them and butter them,
Then eat them while they're hot.